S0-ACU-793

INSIDE THE
OLYMPICS

BY TODD KORTEMEIER

Somerset County Library
Bridgewater, NJ 08807

The Child's World®
childsworld.com

Published by The Child's World®
1980 Lookout Drive • Mankato, MN 56003-1705
800-599-READ • www.childsworld.com

Acknowledgments
The Child's World®: Mary Berendes, Publishing Director
Red Line Editorial: Design, editorial direction, and production
Photographs ©: Doug Mills/AP Images, cover, 1; Pete Niesen/Shutterstock Images, 5;
DPA/Picture-Alliance/DPA/AP Images, 6; AP Images, 9, 20, 23, 25; Martynova Anna/
Shutterstock Images, 10; Sven Simon/Imago/Icon Sportswire, 12; Hoch Zwei/Imago/
Icon Sportswire, 15; EMPICS Sport/Press Association/AP Images, 16; Jim McKnight/AP
Images, 18; Michael Sohn/AP Images, 26; Stefan Matzke/NewSport/Corbis, 29

Copyright © 2016 by The Child's World®
All rights reserved. No part of this book may be reproduced or utilized in any form or
by any means without written permission from the publisher.

ISBN 9781634074377

LCCN 2015946279

Printed in the United States of America
Mankato, MN
December, 2015
PA02283

ABOUT THE AUTHOR
Todd Kortemeier is a writer and journalist from Minneapolis.
He is a graduate of the University of Minnesota's School of
Journalism & Mass Communication.

TABLE OF
CONTENTS

FAST FACTS

When is it? The Summer and Winter Olympic Games take place every four years. They are on different scheduling cycles. The Summer Olympics are usually held in July or August. They happen two years after the Winter Games, which have always taken place in January or February.

How do they qualify? In general, athletes must perform at a certain level before the Olympics. Each country's Olympic Committee sets the standards for their athletes.

What do they play for? The top three athletes or teams in each event win a medal. Third place gets bronze. Second place gets silver. First place gets gold. This started in 1904. Silver was the first-place medal before that.

Where is it? Cities bid to host the Olympics. The process begins ten years in advance. National Olympic Committees (NOCs) select a city in their country for consideration. Cities are chosen based on their facilities. Members of the International Olympic Committee (IOC) then vote on a winner.

When was the first one? The first modern Olympics took place in Athens, Greece. That was in 1896. But the ancient Olympics date back to 776 BC. The first Winter Olympics were in Chamonix, France, in 1924.

How many people go? Millions attend each Olympics. The 2012 Games in London sold 8.2 million tickets.

How many people watch? In 2012, up to 4.8 billion people worldwide were able to watch the Olympics on TV or online.

Chapter 1

THE CREATOR'S PERSPECTIVE: PIERRE DE COUBERTIN

Pierre Frédy loved sports as a child in France.

He also was a huge fan of a novel called *Tom Brown's School Days*. It inspired him. The title character was small. So was Pierre. In the book, Brown is a student at the Rugby School in England. He gains strength by playing sports. He also gains confidence. This helps him stand up to the school bully. The book convinced Pierre. People could better themselves through athletics.

Pierre became the Baron de Coubertin in the 1880s. That was a royal position. He became known as Pierre de Coubertin.

Coubertin was a historian and educator. He studied the ancient Olympic Games of Greece. They gave him an idea. He wanted

◀ Pierre de Coubertin is largely responsible for the formation of the modern Olympic Games.

to re-establish "one of the most noteworthy features of Greek civilization."[1]

The Frenchman believed the ancient Olympics were more than just sports. They also helped educate society. He felt this was missing at the time.

Coubertin started traveling. He studied sports around the world. He did not like what he saw. People did not value overall athleticism. They only cared about their individual sport. The ancient Olympics had stopped in 393 AD. Coubertin feared for his new Games idea.

"Under the risk of seeing athletics degenerate and die for a second time, it became necessary to unify it and purify it," he wrote.[2]

He visited Rugby. It was the school from *Tom Brown's School Days*. He met headmaster Thomas Arnold. Coubertin loved Arnold's formula for athletics in education. Arnold believed in fairness, confidence, and intelligence. These principles were important on and off the field.

Coubertin traveled to an English town in 1890. It was called Much Wenlock. Penny Brookes had invited him. Brookes had been organizing his own Olympics there since 1850. Coubertin

Greek athlete Nikolaos Andriakopoulos (top) won gold in ▶ rope climbing at the first modern Summer Olympics in Athens, Greece.

was thrilled. Various sports were being played. Winners received green wreaths on their heads. It was just like the Games in ancient Greece.

Coubertin invited international representatives to Paris in June 1894. That was the beginning of the IOC. The organization was officially founded later that month. The representatives voted to revive the Games. The modern Olympics would start where they began. Greece's capital, Athens, hosted the 1896 Games.

The Greeks wanted to keep hosting the Games in Athens. But Coubertin wanted them held "in the great capitals of the world"[3] every four years. Today's Olympics still follow that vision. The current Olympic **motto** is "Faster, Higher, Stronger." It was adopted by Coubertin.

"These three words represent a program of moral beauty," he wrote.[4]

Coubertin also designed the famous Olympic rings. They have been on the Olympic flag since 1914. Even the Opening Ceremony closely resembles the Frenchman's original program.

Coubertin passed away in 1937. His heart was buried in the ruins of ancient Olympia.

◄ **Coubertin created the iconic Olympic rings logo that has become instantly recognizable around the world.**

Chapter 2

A TORCHBEARER'S PERSPECTIVE: AUSTRALIA'S CATHY FREEMAN

The Olympic flame travels a long way before the Opening Ceremony.

The first Olympic flame was lit in Greece using the sun's rays. That still happens today. Then the flame goes on a journey called a torch relay. Each one is different. But they all end in each host nation's Olympic Stadium.

The 2000 Summer Olympics were in Sydney, Australia. More than 13,000 people carried the flame during the relay. The flame traveled nearly 21,748 miles (35,000 km) from Olympia to Australia. It was the longest relay in history.

Cathy Freeman was waiting at the Olympic Stadium. She would take the torch up a short flight of stairs. Then she would light the

◀ **Cathy Freeman stands with the Olympic torch during the Opening Ceremony of the 2000 Olympic Games.**

Olympic **cauldron**. She had secretly known that she would be lighting it for three years. There was a lot of pressure. It seemed like the whole country was watching.

The next-to-last person in the relay was Debbie Flintoff-King. She was the most-recent Australian woman to win gold in track. Freeman hoped to be the next. She was the 400-meter world champion. About 110,000 fans packed the Olympic Stadium for the cauldron lighting. They roared when Flintoff-King passed the flame to Freeman.

Freeman was not just a famous athlete. She also was an Aboriginal Australian. They are the native people of the country. They had been treated poorly in Australia at times. Freeman's selection was a historic moment for Aboriginal people. Prime Minister John Howard made that clear in his Olympic welcome message.

"It is the Olympic spirit that informs us that the things that unite nations are far greater than the things that divide them," he said.[5]

Freeman got the torch. She ran up the stairs into a shallow pool. She then bent down and touched the torch to the water's surface. A ring of fire lit around her. The ring then lifted up over her. It revealed the Olympic cauldron. It then began to rise to the top of the stadium. But it stopped after just a few feet.

▲ **Freeman holds up the gold medal she won in the 400 meters in front of home fans at the 2000 Olympic Games.**

There was a problem. Freeman stood there for almost four minutes. She waited for the cauldron to move. It finally moved all the way up. The Games could officially begin.

"I have never felt emotion like that before," Freeman later said. "I knew I was going to cry the moment I stepped into the arena with the Australian team. I was just emotionally overwhelmed by the honor of being chosen."[6]

Freeman did win gold in the 400 meters. Her legacy lives on at Cathy Freeman Park in Sydney. It is the 2012 cauldron's permanent home.

Chapter 3

THE FANS' PERSPECTIVE: LONDON OLYMPICS FANS

Athletes are the focus of every Olympics. They come from various countries to compete. But fans also come from across the globe. Some of them have a sport of their own. It is the "sport" of pin trading.

Many organizations, including NOCs and sponsors, make pins for each Olympics. They are handed out or sold at the Games.

Trading these pins brings people together. It helps them learn about other cultures. American Don Bigsby was the president of a pin collectors club. He had more than 100,000 himself.

"I've been to 14 Olympics and I can't stop," he said at the London 2012 Olympic Games.[7]

Pierre de Coubertin wanted sports to bring people together. That idea lives on at the Olympics. Irwin Gabriel Lopez attended a

◀ Unique pins, such as these from London 2012, are made for each edition of the Olympic Games.

▲ **Don Bigsby founded the Olympin Collectors Club, known as the world's biggest Olympic memorabilia club.**

basketball game in London. Russia and Spain were playing. Fans of both teams were there. Other attendees just loved basketball.

"The Olympic atmosphere was awesome. I had the time of my life," Lopez said. "The crowd spoke all kinds of languages. But we all understood each other. We knew when to cheer/boo and what to cheer/boo for."[8]

Amanda Williams is a former gymnast. It was her dream to see Olympic gymnastics live in person. She got her chance in 2012.

"The city was absolutely electric with an energy and spirit that can only go hand-in-hand with an international event like the Olympic Games," she said. "I felt like I was a part of something— something big."[9]

Harry Nelson attended his 18th Summer Olympics in 2012. That was his second in London. He had sold his car to make it to the 1948 London Games. And he had brought his children to the 1972 Munich and 1976 Montreal Games.

"Just seeing all the Olympic events was just really neat," his son Chad said. "There's always a source of pride when you know your nation finishes first, and you hear the national anthem."[10]

The Games have changed a lot since 1932. That was the year of Harry's first Olympics. He turned 90 in 2012. But he had no plans to stop traveling to the Games.

"It's my hobby, and as long as we can do it, we will," he said.[11]

Chapter 4

A COACH'S PERSPECTIVE: THE U.S.A.'S HERB BROOKS

The 1980 United States hockey team knew what it was up against. The Soviet Union was the best team in the world. It had won four straight golds prior to 1980.

The players on the U.S. team had seen the Soviets' skill firsthand. The United States had played them in an **exhibition** match just days before the Olympics. The United States lost 10–3.

American Herb Brooks had coached the University of Minnesota. He won three national championships there. But the Olympics were a different challenge. He selected the U.S. team in 1979. It played 61 warm-up games.

The United States was ranked seventh coming into the Games in Lake Placid, New York. But the team went undefeated in the first round. That got the United States to the medal round. The Soviets were waiting.

◀ Coach Herb Brooks (right) skates with goalie Jim Craig during practice on February 21, 1980.

There was more than just hockey at stake. The United States and the Soviet Union were at odds politically. It was the height of the Cold War. The two nations never officially declared war on each other. But there was a lot of tension between them.

Brooks wanted the players to believe in themselves. He read them a note before the game. He had written exactly what he wanted to say.

"You were born to be a player. You were meant to be here at this moment. You were meant to be here at this game," Brooks said.[12]

The U.S. team took the ice. The sold-out crowd was loud and supportive. People waved flags and chanted, "U.S.A.! U.S.A.!"[13]

It looked like the Soviets would finish the first period leading 2–1. But U.S. forward Mark Johnson tied the game just a few seconds before the break.

The Soviets changed their goaltender. People were shocked. Vladislav Tretiak was considered the strongest goalie in the world. But Vladimir Myshkin was brought in. Soviet coach Viktor Tikhonov would later call it, "the biggest mistake of my career."[14]

The Soviets dominated the second period. But they only scored once. It was 3–2 going into the final period.

The United States celebrates after its historic upset of the ▶ Soviet Union.

"I stressed we must stay with our system and our **tactics**," Brooks said later. "I've seen too many teams back off from the Soviets."[15]

The United States came out determined in the third. It tied the game with a **power-play** goal. Then the unthinkable happened. The Americans took the lead 81 seconds later.

They were close to **upsetting** the best hockey team in the world. Brooks tried to keep his team under control.

"Play your game!" Brooks shouted from the bench.[16]

The Soviets spent most of the last minute in the U.S. **zone**. The United States desperately hung on. With five seconds left, the Americans cleared the puck out of their zone. The final seconds ticked away and the buzzer sounded. The United States had beaten the Soviets 4–3.

Afterward, the players celebrated with the American flag. They sang "God Bless America" in the locker room. And Brooks got a very important phone call.

"[U.S.] President [Jimmy] Carter said we made the American people very proud," Brooks said.[17]

The two countries were in conflict off the ice. There were serious threats being made by both sides. But that was not the case that night at the Lake Placid Olympic Center. That night it was just a hockey game.

▲ Brooks (on phone) receives a phone call from U.S. President Jimmy Carter after the 4–3 win over the Soviet Union.

"The fans displayed excellent sportsmanship, even though we have different ways of life and different government[s]," Brooks said. "There was no politics on behalf of the Russians and no politics by us."[18]

Chapter 5

AN ATHLETE'S PERSPECTIVE: THE U.S.A.'S MICHAEL PHELPS

Swimmer Michael Phelps was preparing for his second Olympics. It was 2004. He had made his Games debut at the Sydney 2000 Games. Phelps had been just 15. He did not medal. But he showed promise.

Big things were expected of him at Athens 2004. People thought he could challenge Mark Spitz's record. Spitz had won seven swimming gold medals at Munich 1972. Even Spitz thought Phelps could do it. But Phelps was not thinking that far ahead.

"To stand up on that **podium** and hear the national anthem would be awesome," Phelps said.[19]

He won six gold and two bronze medals. He just missed Spitz's record. But it was the second-best Olympics performance ever.

◀ **U.S. swimmer Michael Phelps holds his gold medal for the 100-meter butterfly at the 2012 Olympic Games.**

Even as a young swimmer, it was Phelps's goal to be one of the best ever.

"When Michael was 15, he told me he wanted to change the sport of swimming," Cathy Lears, one of Phelps's early instructors, said. "It was like, 'yeah, right, who told you to say that, kid?' But he's always had a vision that swimming could become important to American fans."[20]

Many American eyes focused on Phelps at Beijing 2008. Those Games were the most-watched in American history at the time. Phelps was a big reason why. He won eight gold medals. That broke Spitz's record.

It was going to be a hard act to follow. Phelps considered retiring. He took some time off. But then he trained hard for London 2012. He had a chance to become the greatest Olympian of all time.

Phelps won four golds and two silvers. That brought his career Olympic medal total to 22. It broke Soviet gymnast Larisa Latynina's record of 18. He was honored with a trophy.

"It's kind of weird looking at this and seeing 'Greatest Olympian of All Time,'" Phelps said.[21]

Phelps said he was retiring. But he changed his mind. In 2015, he announced he would try to compete at Rio de Janeiro 2016.

▲ Phelps won his first Olympic gold medal in the 400-meter individual medley at the 2004 Games.

Phelps loves being an Olympian. He has always stayed in the Olympic Village. That gives him the full Olympics experience.

"Being able to be in the same exact environment as people from all over the world, and . . . the best athletes from all over the world coming together, I think, is something you don't find at any other place but the Olympic Games," Phelps said. "That's something that's exciting for me to be a part of."[22]

GLOSSARY

cauldron (KAWL-druhn): A cauldron is a large bowl or vessel. Cathy Freeman lit the Olympic cauldron in 2000.

exhibition (ex-ih-BISH-un): An exhibition match is a game that does not officially count and is often used for practice. The Soviet Union beat the United States 10–3 in an exhibition hockey game before the 1980 Olympics.

motto (MAH-toe): A motto is an official saying and summary of an organization's mission. The Olympic motto is "Faster, Higher, Stronger."

podium (POE-dee-uhm): A podium is a small stage with three levels where the top three finishers stand to receive their medals. Michael Phelps dreamed of standing atop the podium.

power-play (POU-er pley): A power-play goal occurs in hockey when a team scores while the opposing team has a player in the penalty box. The United States scored a power-play goal in the third period of its game against the Soviet Union in 1980.

tactics (TACK-ticks): Tactics are strategies teams use during a game. Coach Herb Brooks reminded the U.S. hockey players to keep their tactics in mind when playing the Soviet Union.

upsetting (uhp-SET-ing): Upsetting a team is beating it when it is supposed to beat you. The U.S. hockey team was on its way to upsetting the Soviet Union late in the third period.

zone (zohn): In hockey, a zone is an end of the ice where a team is either on offense or defense. The Soviet Union spent much of the final minute in the U.S. zone in the teams' famous 1980 Olympic hockey game.

SOURCE NOTES

1-3. Pierre de Coubertin. "The Olympic Games: Athens 1896." *Olympic-Legacy.* Olympic-Legacy. n.d. Web. 6 May 2015.

4. "Olympic Report." *Olympic.org.* International Olympic Committee. n.d. Web. 21 May 2015.

5. "Official Report of the XXVII Olympiad Volume Two: Celebrating the Games." *LA84.* LA84 Foundation. n.d. Web. 21 May 2015.

6. Richard Sandomir. "Sydney 2000: Notebook; Freeman's Emotional Moment." *New York Times.* The New York Times Company. 17 Sep. 2000. Web. 21 May 2015.

7. Jake Whitman. "In Olympic Sport of Pin Trading, Anyone Can 'Medal'." *ABC News.* ABC News. 8 Aug. 2012. Web. 21 May 2015.

8. Irwin Gabriel Lopez. "Scholar's London 2012 Olympic Experience." *Chevening.* Crown of the United Kingdom. 2 Aug. 2013. Web. 21 May 2015.

9. Amanda Williams. "London 2012: My Olympics Experience." *A Dangerous Business.* A Dangerous Business Travel Blog. 13 Aug. 2012. Web. 21 May 2015.

10-11. Caroline Tan. "For Torrance Resident, London 2012 Marks 18th Time at Summer Olympics." *NBC Los Angeles.* NBCUniversal Media. 27 Jul. 2012. Web. 21 May 2015.

12-13. Dave Kindred. "Born to Be Players, Born to the Moment." *Washington Post.* The Washington Post Company. 23 Feb. 1980. Web. 22 May 2015.

14. Wayne Coffey. "Viktor Tikhonov Coached Russia to Three Olympic Gold Medals, but Is Remembered for Losing 'Miracle' Game in 1980." *New York Daily News.* New York Daily News. 25 Nov. 2014. Web. 29 Jun. 2015.

15. Leonard Shapiro. "U.S. Shocks Soviets in Ice Hockey, 4-3." *Washington Post.* The Washington Post Company. 23 Feb. 1980. Web. 22 May 2015.

16-18. Dave Kindred. 23 Feb. 1980.

19. Tim Layden. "Hold Your Breath." *Sports Illustrated.* Time Inc. 2 Aug. 2004. Web. 22 May 2015.

20. "Sportsman of the Year: Michael Phelps." *Sports Illustrated.* Time Inc. 2 Dec. 2008. Web. 22 May 2015.

21-22. Bill Chappell. "Michael Phelps Exits the Olympics, and Enters Retirement at 27." *npr.* npr. 12 Aug. 2012. Web. 22 May 2015.

TO LEARN MORE

Books

Christopher, Matt. *Great Moments in the Summer Olympics.* New York: Little, Brown, and Co., 2012.

Gifford, Clive. *So You Think You Know the Olympics.* London: Hodder Children's Books, 2011.

Macy, Sue. *Freeze Frame: A Photographic History of the Winter Olympics.* Washington, DC: National Geographic, 2006.

Web Sites

Visit our Web site for links about the Olympics: childsworld.com/links

Note to Parents, Teachers, and Librarians: We routinely verify our Web links to make sure they are safe and active sites. So encourage your readers to check them out!

INDEX

J 796.48 KOR

Kortemeier, Todd, 1986–

Inside the Olympics

APR 2 8 2016